For my beloved granddaughters, Alexandra and Kelli,
who introduced me to the original "mad dog."

With special thanks to Sue Tarsky
who was the first to believe.   —M. U.

For all my Monks and Tobin relatives in America.   —L. M.

Text copyright © 2000 by Myron Uhlberg. Illustrations copyright © 2000 by Lydia Monks
All rights reserved. This book, or parts thereof, may not be reproduced
in any form without permission in writing from the publisher.
G. P. Putnam's Sons, a division of Penguin Putnam Books for Young Readers,
345 Hudson Street, New York, NY 10014. G. P. Putnam's Sons, Reg. U.S. Pat. & Tm. Off.
Published simultaneously in Canada. Printed in Hong Kong by South China Printing Co. (1988) Ltd.
Designed by Marikka Tamura. Text set in Malloy.
The illustrations were created with acrylic paint, paper montage, and colored pencils.
Library of Congress Cataloging-in-Publication Data
Uhlberg, Myron.   Mad Dog McGraw / Myron Uhlberg : illustrations by Lydia Monks.
p. cm.   Summary: After trying many tricks, a young boy finally figures out how
to deal with the meanest dog in the neighborhood.
ISBN 0-399-23308-3 [1. Dogs—Fiction.] I. Monks, Lydia, ill.   II. Title.
PZ7.U3255Mad 2000 [E]—dc21 98-41169 CIP AC
10 9 8 7 6 5 4 3 2 1
First Impression

MAD DOG McGRAW

MYRON UHLBERG

ILLUSTRATIONS BY LYDIA MONKS

G. P. PUTNAM'S SONS   NEW YORK

I hate Mad Dog McGraw!

He barks like crazy, and he chases me.

He growls at trucks.

He snaps at clouds.

He barks at rain.

He shows his teeth to the wind.

He is one mean dog.

The mailman is afraid to
leave the mail next door.

The milkman won't deliver their milk.
The paperboy throws their paper.

And when I see Mad Dog, I go the other way.
He is one mean dog.

"I need stilts," I tell Mom. "Mad Dog tries to bite me."

"But honey, you don't know how to walk on stilts."

"I'll learn fast."

I find two old broom handles and make stilts.

I practice all week.
I'm ready for Mad Dog McGraw.

Here he comes.
He snaps.
He yelps.
He jumps.
But he can't reach me.
I've tricked Mad Dog McGraw!

Then my left stilt gets
caught in a crack.

Mad Dog McGraw chases me home.
I think I hear him laughing in between his barks.
He is one mean dog.

"I need an umbrella," I tell Mom. "I'm going to sail right over Mad Dog McGraw."

"But sweetheart, you can't fly."

"I'll learn fast."

I practice all week. On Saturday, there's a strong wind blowing. I grab my umbrella. I'm ready for Mad Dog McGraw.

The wind is gusting. I open my umbrella and off I go.

Mad Dog spots me.

He hops.

He skips.

He jumps.

But he can't reach me.

I've tricked Mad Dog McGraw!

Then the wind stops.

Mad Dog McGraw chases me home.
I'm pretty sure he's laughing again.

He is
one
mean
dog.

"I need a cat,"
I tell Mom.

"But darling,
we don't
have
a cat."

"I'll find a stray."

Dad and I put down a saucer of milk.
Soon I have a cat. I call her Bait.

Bait and I tiptoe past Mad Dog McGraw's house.
Mad Dog gnashes those teeth.

Mad Dog leaps.

Bait purrs.

Bait licks Mad Dog's face.
Mad Dog nuzzles Bait.

Mad Dog chases me home.
This time I know he's laughing.

He is one mean dog.

Mom is waiting for me.

"Well, Mom,
that didn't work.
Mad Dog is still mean."

"I wonder why?"
Mom says.

I think about it.
And then
I think
some more.
Tricks don't seem to work.

All night I think about it. And then
I remember what happened with Bait.
Now I get it.
I'm learning fast.

The next morning, I go right to Mad Dog McGraw's house.
I know I don't need stilts, or an umbrella, or Bait.

I sit back on my heels.
I don't know who's more surprised,
Mad Dog or me.

I smile and hold out
a dog biscuit.

Mad Dog comes closer.
He sniffs.
He sniffs some more.
He looks at me and takes the treat.
He comes even closer.

He sniffs me.
He sniffs some more.

He sits, and I rub his head.
He licks my hand.

I know absolutely for a fact that
Mad Dog is smiling.

I stand.
Mad Dog McGraw stands.
I walk home.

Mad Dog McGraw follows,
with Bait not far behind.

I think he is
one great dog.

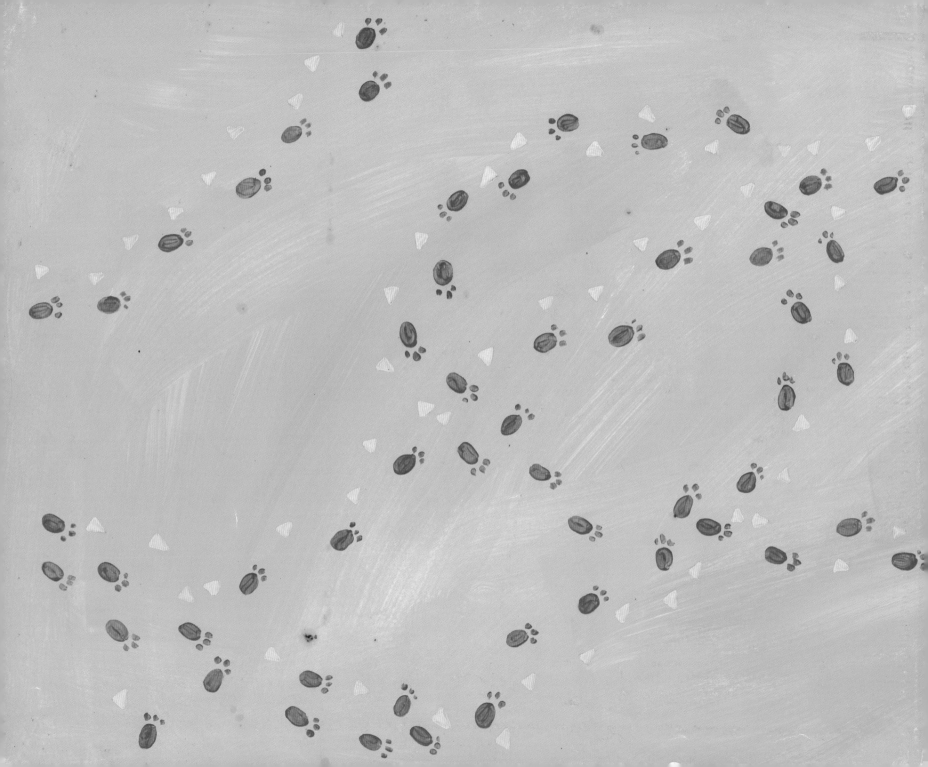